# Ollie and Claire

Tiffany Strelitz Haber • Matthew Cordell

PHILOMEL BOOKS • An Imprint of Penguin Group (USA) Inc.

# Philomel Books

A division of Penguin Young Readers Group.   Published by The Penguin Group.

Penguin Group (USA) Inc., 375 Hudson Street, New York, NY 10014, U.S.A.

Penguin Group (Canada), 90 Eglinton Avenue East, Suite 700, Toronto, Ontario M4P 2Y3, Canada
(a division of Pearson Penguin Canada Inc.).

Penguin Books Ltd, 80 Strand, London WC2R 0RL, England.

Penguin Ireland, 25 St. Stephen's Green, Dublin 2, Ireland (a division of Penguin Books Ltd).

Penguin Group (Australia), 250 Camberwell Road, Camberwell, Victoria 3124, Australia
(a division of Pearson Australia Group Pty Ltd).

Penguin Books India Pvt Ltd, 11 Community Centre, Panchsheel Park, New Delhi - 110 017, India.

Penguin Group (NZ), 67 Apollo Drive, Rosedale, Auckland 0632, New Zealand (a division of Pearson New Zealand Ltd).

Penguin Books (South Africa) (Pty) Ltd, 24 Sturdee Avenue, Rosebank, Johannesburg 2196, South Africa.

Penguin Books Ltd, Registered Offices: 80 Strand, London WC2R 0RL, England.

Design by Semadar Megged.   Edited by Tamra Tuller.
Text set in 17-point ITC Legacy Sans.   The illustrations in this book were created using pencil (with a hint of digital magic) and watercolor.

Library of Congress Cataloging-in-Publication Data
Haber, Tiffany Strelitz.   Ollie and Claire / Tiffany Strelitz Haber ; illustrated by Matthew Cordell.   p. cm.
Summary: Bored with her ho-hum routine with her best friend Ollie, Claire secretly plans a new adventure with a mystery person.
[1. Stories in rhyme. 2. Best friends—Fiction. 3. Friendship—Fiction. 4. Dogs—Fiction.] I. Cordell, Matthew, 1975- ill. II. Title.
PZ8.3.H1156Oll 2013   [E]—dc23   2011049771   ISBN 978-0-399-25603-5

10 9 8 7 6 5 4 3 2 1

To Jack Dalton and Travis Hawk. May your lives
be a beautiful adventure!
Love you forever,
Mommy

For Julie and Romy.
—M.C.

Ollie and Claire were a tightly knit pair,
like hot buttered biscuits and jam.

They frolicked by day at the park and the bay,
where they yodeled and yoga'd and swam.

Nap time, then snack time, then off-to-the-track time
to practice their hurdles and run.
Three times around, till they both hit the ground

and collapsed in the heat of the sun.

Dinner each night: bologna on white, promptly at 7:15.
But Claire was aware that she needed a change.

"I'm bored with this ho-hum routine."

Early one Friday, while taking a stroll, she spotted a sign on a tree:

Claire started dreaming of pirate-ship
sightings and meeting a mermaid or two.

"Ollie won't mind if I leave him behind—
this is nothing he *ever* would do."

"Off to the mountains!
Off to the moon!"
In her head she was
starting to pack.

"Off to the trip of a
lifetime!" she cheered,
and quickly composed a
note back.

*I'd love to discover where lollipops grow . . .*
*where dinosaurs rumble and roar.*
*I'm ready and willing, let's go go go go!*
*See you here Monday at 4.*

Claire hurried home, where she tore through the closets
and gathered up all of her things:
a hat and some pants that were perfect for France,
pajamas and pink water wings,

toe shoes and snowshoes and go-with-the-flow shoes,
a thingamajig and a kit.
She squished and she pushed and she mushed it all in,
and then zipped it right up, and it fit!

Later that evening, her telephone rang.
It was Ollie, and oddly enough,

he said, "I can't play for a couple of days . . .
I've got to take care of some stuff."

Claire spent the weekend alone on her boat,
to dream of the journey ahead,
she mused as she rowed, but her mind overflowed
with visions of Ollie instead.

Afloat on the lake: "Is this trip a mistake?"
Claire wasn't sure she could go.
Heading to shore: "I can't wait anymore . . .
there's something that Ollie should know."

She penned him a note. *I'm so sorry,* she wrote.
*And maybe you aren't aware . . .*
*But I'm going away, and I'll miss you each day,*

*and I hope you'll forgive me. Love, Claire.*

On Monday at 4, she collected her luggage
and made her way down to the tree.
Anxiously pacing, her nervous heart racing,
she wondered just who it would be.

When out from the willows, a figure appeared . . .

"My gosh, could it really be true?"
She wasn't prepared for this kind of surprise.
"Oh, Ollie, is that really YOU?!"

"Well, let me just say, and I hope it's okay,
for whatever you think this is worth—"

"I'm SO glad it's you!"
"I'm so glad it's you, too!"

And they set off to travel the earth!